Buck's Bad Dreams

by Michael Scotto

illustrated by The Ink Circle

WELCOME TO MIDLANDIA
OUR STORY BEGINS

Midlandia University

Community Center

Animal Land

HERE

Town Square

Playland Park

Bike Factory

Harvest Farms

STARRING
P.T. O. BoBo
THE RINGMASTER

BUCK O. BOBO
THE
BANKER &
PHILANTHROPIST

Buck the banker liked to give money back to his community, Midlandia. Those who care for and give back to their communities are called philanthropists.

Buck was proud to be a philanthropist. Partly, he liked having such a long and hard-to-spell title. He especially enjoyed signing letters. "Sincerely," he would write, "Buck O. Bobo, banker and **philanthropist.**"

BUCK O. BOBO
BANKER AND PHILANTHROPIST

But even more, Buck enjoyed seeing Midlandians smile after he had helped them. **"Thank you so much!"** said P.T., the circus owner. "With your donation, I can finally get that third ring for my next show!"

"I'll be in the front row on opening night," Buck promised.

And that was how
the trouble began.

Buck loved P.T.'s show at first. He marveled at the flying trapezes, juggling clowns, and P.T.'s fantastic tumbling.

But then...

"Ladies and gentle-Midlandians," P.T. announced,
"I introduce our newest act, made possible by Mr.
Buck O. Bobo! Please welcome to the center ring,
Larry the Leaping Lion!"

The whole audience clapped wildly—
everyone except for Buck. Buck was frozen
with fear. "That lion is huge," he thought.
"He could swallow me whole!"

"Tonight," P.T. declared, "Larry will leap
through the famed hoop of fire!" This got
Buck really scared. He did not like fire one bit.

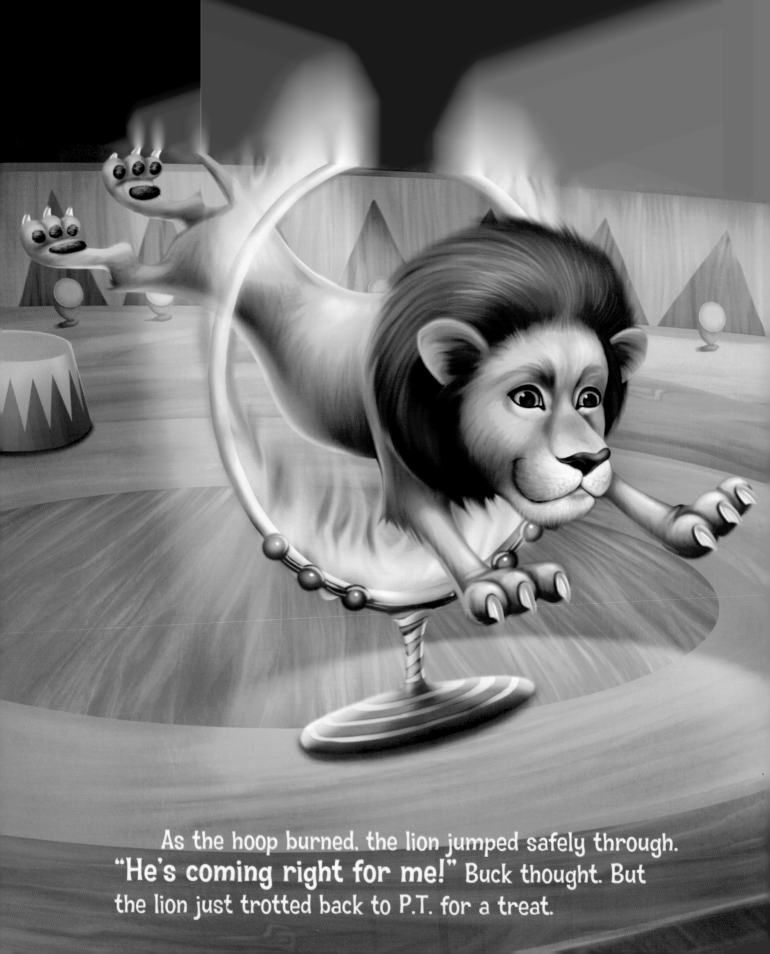

As the hoop burned, the lion jumped safely through.
"He's coming right for me!" Buck thought. But
the lion just trotted back to P.T. for a treat.

Buck could not take any more scares. As everyone clapped. he sprinted all the way home and hid underneath his covers.

That night, Buck heard a low growling sound. "How did I get here?" Buck thought, puzzled. "I went to sleep at home, but now I'm back at the circus!" He heard the growling again.

It was P.T.'s lion! He was even bigger than before. Buck looked for somewhere to hide, and he saw something strange. "My bank vault!" he thought. "That looks safe." He hurried for the vault, but out of nowhere, a ring of fire appeared in his way! "I'm trapped," Buck whispered. **Just before the lion pounced...**

Buck woke up, safe in his bed.
"It was only a bad dream," he sighed.

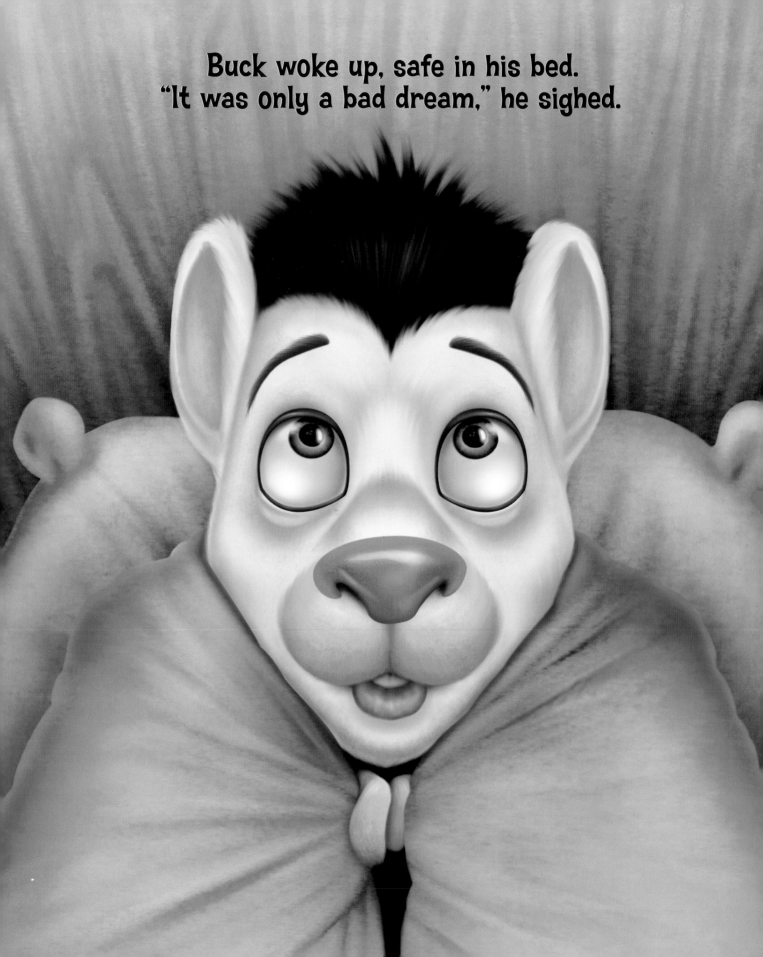

Buck was tired the next day—tired and grouchy.
He had not slept a wink since his bad dream. Soon, P.T.
stopped by the bank to visit. "I missed you after the
show," P.T. said. **"How did you like my new act?"**

Buck remembered his dream and, suddenly, he grew
very angry. "Your lion was lousy, and so was your show!"
Buck yelled. **"In fact, I want my donation back."**

P.T. was shocked. "Without your help, I'll have to close
the circus," he said.

"That's exactly the idea," Buck said.

After P.T. left, Buck felt guilty. He did not like hurting his friend. "If P.T.'s show is gone, though, maybe my bad dreams will go away, too," he thought.

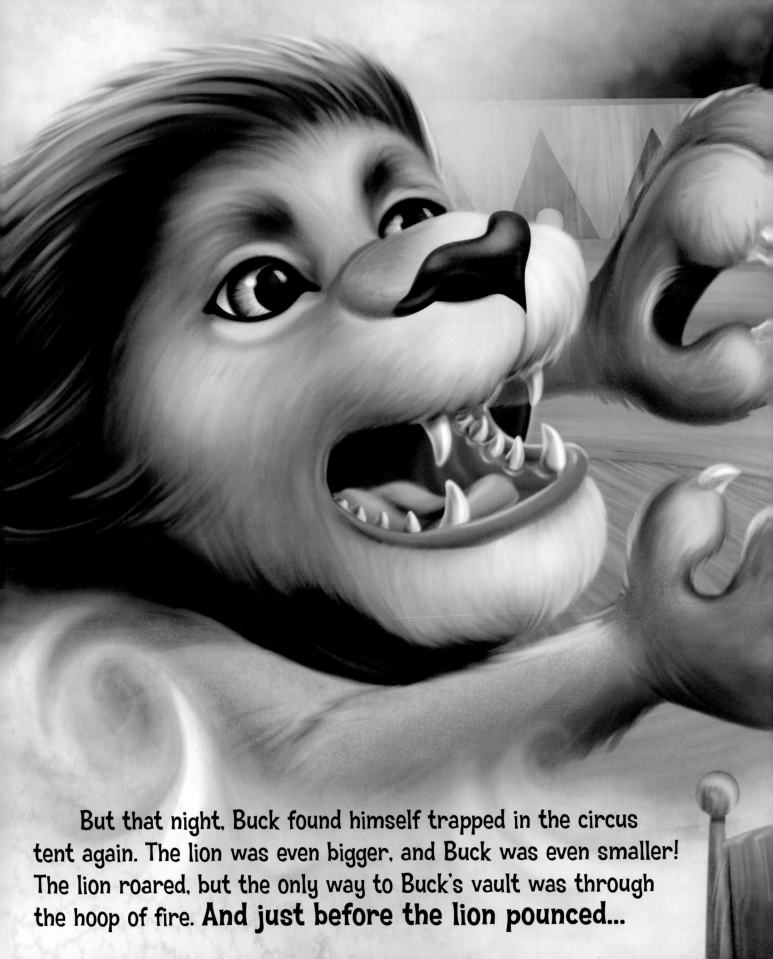

But that night, Buck found himself trapped in the circus tent again. The lion was even bigger, and Buck was even smaller! The lion roared, but the only way to Buck's vault was through the hoop of fire. **And just before the lion pounced...**

Buck woke up shivering in his bed. "What is wrong with me?" he wondered.

In the morning, Buck went for a walk. "I don't get it," he said. "I made P.T. close his show, but I'm still having bad dreams." **Soon, he found himself at P.T.'s circus tent.**

Inside, Buck saw P.T. packing up. "What are you doing here?" P.T. asked.

"I should not have made you close your show," Buck said. "I was not being a good philanthropist, or a good friend. I'm **really sorry.**"

"Why did you get mad at me?" P.T. asked.

"Your circus lion really scared me," Buck admitted. "Then I started having bad dreams about it, and I blamed you. I am so embarrassed."

"Bad dreams are nothing to be embarrassed about," P.T. said. "One time, I dreamt that I went out to perform wearing nothing but my underwear!"

"You have bad dreams?" Buck asked.

"Everyone has bad dreams sometimes," P.T. said. "Dreams come from things you see and things that you are thinking about. They are like stories that you make up without even knowing it. When you have a bad dream, you only need to change the story."

"How can I do that?" Buck asked.

"When you go to bed, think about fun things that you'd like to dream about—things that make you happy," P.T. suggested. "If you've had a bad dream, think about how you'd change it to make it a good dream. That usually helps me."

That night, Buck took P.T.'s advice. Soon, he found himself having another circus dream...but this time it was a little different. Buck saw the hoop of fire, but he did not let it scare him. He just clapped his hands and, in an instant, it turned into a ring of jewels and coins. **"That's much better!"** Buck said as he jumped through the ring.

P.T.'s lion ran toward Buck. But as it got closer, Buck saw the lion shrink and turn into a lion cub before his eyes. The little cub jumped into Buck's arms. **"You aren't scary at all!"** Buck said as he petted the cub.

Buck could still hear the cub's purring when he awoke. The moment he got to the bank, he sat down to write P.T. a thank you note.

BUCK O. BOBO
BANKER AND PHILANTHROPIST

"Dear P.T.," Buck began. "**You were right.** I don't have to let bad dreams get me down. I'll come see your show again soon (but maybe not from the front row). Your friend, Buck O. Bobo." He smiled, and then quickly added, "**banker and philanthropist.**"

DISCUSSION QUESTIONS

Have you ever had a bad dream before?
What was your dream about?
Who helps you when you have bad dreams?

Philanthropists do not always give money to their communities. What are some other ways that you can contribute to the area where you live?